The Gr

Also by M.A.C. Farrant

Short Fiction

Novels

Non-Fiction

Plays

*Available from Talonbooks

The Great Happiness

Stories and Comics

M.A.C. Farrant

Talonbooks

Talonbooks
9259 Shaughnessy Street, Vancouver, British Columbia, Canada v6p 6r4
talonbooks.com

Talonbooks is located on xʷməθkʷəy̓əm, Sḵwx̱wú7mesh, and
səl̓ilwətaʔɬ Lands.

First printing: 2019
Typeset in Scala

Printed and bound in Canada on 100% post-consumer recycled paper

Cover illustration by Catrin Welz-Stein, catrinwelzstein.blogspot.com
Cover design by Chloë Filson
Interior design by Chloë Filson and andrea bennett
Comic illustrations by andrea bennett

Talonbooks gratefully acknowledges the financial support of the
Canada Council for the Arts, the Government of Canada through the
Canada Book Fund, and the Province of British Columbia through the
British Columbia Arts Council and the Book Publishing Tax Credit.

LIBRARY AND ARCHIVES CANADA CATALOGUING IN PUBLICATION

Farrant, M. A. C. (Marion Alice Coburn), author
        The great happiness : stories and comics / by M.A.C. Farrant.

Short stories.
Illustrated by andrea bennett.
ISBN 978-1-77201-221-7 (SOFTCOVER)

        I. bennett, andrea, illustrator II. Title.

PS8561.A76C74 2019   c813'.54   c2018.906434-x

For Vicky

*She saved a rock about to fall
from a ledge.*

*She found some socks thrown
into a corner.*

—James Tate

Contents

I

2

I

Positive Impact

On Saturday, July 9, 2016, Buddhist monks from the Great Enlightenment Buddhist Institute, in Little Sands, PEI, bought six hundred pounds of live lobsters from several establishments and returned them to the ocean, thus saving the lobsters' lives. It was, the monks said, an act of compassion.

When she heard this, a woman from the West Coast was inspired to rescue the last northern lobster from her town's Save-On-Foods, where it had been languishing for several days at the bottom of a display tank. She'd noticed it while shopping and worried about its future. Now she had a plan. She purchased the lobster and carried it home in a pail half-filled with water from the tank. The next day she shipped the lobster via Purolator, at a cost of 245 dollars, to her friend in Prince Edward Island with the instruction that, like the Buddhists' lobsters, hers would be returned to the ocean.

"It's a spiritual thing," she explained to the local TV station when the news broke. "Sometimes spirituality gets so structured it doesn't even feel like you're living."

It was a Purolator agent who tipped off the TV station. He told them the story "just translated" for him and that he found it "real and soulful."

"It's an example of being a little better than you are," he said.

The Weather Channel

"I won't lie to you," the woman was telling her daughter. "There have been train wrecks. I've lived in suspended adolescence for much of my life. But then, when I turned sixty, things started to calm down and a low-grade happiness took over. I'm not sure why. Getting older maybe. Getting that big payout from your dad."

"Don't talk about Dad," said the daughter.

They were having drinks in the Dockside Pub after the daughter's shift at Starbucks.

"Okay, but this is important," her mother continued. "It's something you need to know. Very quietly, very slowly, happiness can take over a person's life. It happened to me. Not a big kind of happiness with streamers and balloons, more of a background happiness, like the music you hear on the Weather Channel."

"Seriously," said the daughter.

"When I hear that music," the mother said, "I think: This perfectly describes the way my happiness feels. Light and kind of spacey."

"The Weather Channel."

"Yes. And now when I notice other people, older ones like myself, walking down the street, going about their business, and having these little smiles on their faces, I know they're plugged into the Weather Channel too. Everyone enjoying the same kind of quiet happiness that I am."

"Well, *he's* not happy," the daughter said.

"Who?"

"Dad. All he ever does is come home from work, crack a beer, and complain about the government."

Hearing this caused the women to feel slightly happier than she usually felt.

But in fairness to the girl's father and feeling a little guilty because she enjoyed hearing about her ex's misery, she said, "Nevertheless, a happy woman like me can still find things to be unhappy about."

"Like what?"

"Well, I'm very wary that I won't last forever."

"Mother!"

"Just kidding."

Pie

"Ah, man, it's sad," the man was saying to his friend. "The pie is never going to be very large. My share of it will always be small."

As usual, he was sitting on a camp chair outside the town's post office working on his beading, this time a design of a brown and black dog. He'd placed a large bowl containing a few coins near his feet.

His friend, who was heavyset, crouched down with difficulty. "Yeah," he said. "Life's a bitch." He was licking a strawberry ice cream cone.

"It's the nature of my time here," the man continued. "It won't be particularly profound or important to anyone but myself."

Their conversation was interrupted when the man looked up and said "Have a nice day" to a passerby who'd just tossed some change into his bowl.

The friend wandered off towards the pier.

It was a hot July afternoon and the man continued working in the shade of the building. A few more people threw change into his bowl and a few more times he looked up and said, "Have a nice day."

Then around four, two elderly women approached him with a small blackberry and apple pie.

"This is for you," they said. Privately, they called the man the Bead Man. They thought of him as a pleasant and deserving person. Surprised, the man accepted the pie.

The women were from the church a block over, two of a group of seniors making pies in the church basement as a fundraiser. They'd had some leftover pastry dough and some extra fruit and they'd decided to make a few small pies for the town's less fortunate. There was a pie for Lena, the woman who roamed the

Avenue collecting bottles and cans in a grocery cart; there was one for Marilyn, the stroke victim, who was always seen pushing a walker and smoking a cigarette, and who had once, as a volunteer, fed a hockey team in her kitchen. There was a pie for Brian, the old artist, who was often sitting on the Avenue bench beside the bronze statue of a fisherman.

"We love helping people," the women said after delivering the pies, including one to the man playing guitar outside the bookstore because they couldn't find Marilyn.

An Attempt to Love the Moment

The cat was stretched out in the sun and there were new grass, cherry and magnolia blossoms to view. They were having drinks on the back deck, trying to enjoy a rare day off from their window-covering business.

For a while they watched sparrows darting in and out of climbing rose vines, gathering material for their nests. Then they watched the retired forensic pathologist who lived next door – a pleasant man, always eager to leave a person smiling. He was practising golf swings on his back lawn. Eventually he hit a golf ball to the bottom of his yard where it landed beside a flowering plum. He retrieved the ball, got into position, practised a few more swings, and then hit the ball again. This hit-and-retrieve manoeuvre lasted for half an hour.

That day he was wearing a light blue sweater and grey cords from the town's best store. He'd retired at fifty-five on his investments, the murderers and those who were murdered now thirty years behind him.

Their neighbour had ascended to a life of golf after a long mystical climb, the couple understood, and was deeply happy.

The complexity of this situation continues to attack them.

Spontaneity, Danger, Passion

There's a deer problem in our area. Each year more and more deer wander into people's gardens and eat their vegetable plants, roses, flowering shrubs. They arrive in early morning or at dusk, three or four of them, old and young, and if you shout at them to leave they turn and look at you curiously, as if to ask, "Was there something you wanted?"

As a gesture of community service, a gentle couple – she's a retired pharmacist, she's a retired healthcare worker – have taken to canvassing the neighbourhood for donations to fund sterilizing the males.

We imagine their idea is to set up a MASH unit in their carport and that they'll need equipment – a tranquillizer gun, dolly, hoist, bandages, books on castration techniques.

"The nature of our fight may not seem earth-shattering," they tell us, standing on our doorstep with their collection jar, "but this is the modern world. We do what we can."

The Happy Places

"It needs to be pointed out," the old man was saying to passersby. He was huddled beneath the overhang of a building and paused to take a drag off his cigarette. Rain was coming down hard.

"It needs to be said," he continued, "that wherever you go in the world, where you are still allowed to smoke cigarettes in licensed premises, those are the happy places."

The Humorist

I was walking along the town's main street – the
Avenue – on a warm afternoon and bumped into Ron
and Dorothy Root outside the jewellery store. I've known
them for years. They're both in their seventies. Right
away Ron said, "How does it feel to be an orphan?"

Dorothy, who is much shorter than Ron, tilted her
head back and shouted, "Pardon?"

Ron ignored her and spoke to me. "Your parents are
dead, right? So you're an orphan."

"Yes, I suppose I am," I said. "They've been dead
for years."

"You see!" Ron said, turning to his wife. "We're
all orphans!"

This made Dorothy mad. "Excuse me!" she
shouted. "Why are we talking about death on a beautiful
May afternoon?"

It's well known in town that Ron is something of a
humorist. One January a few years ago in Pharmasave,
he told me that Christmas was better now because
the last of the family drunks had died. I thought
that was funny.

But I didn't think his comment about orphans
was funny; instead, I thought it fell flat. Now I wonder
if his powers as a humorist are waning, his weak joke
indicating that he's suffering from something, well,
grave. When that happens, as everyone knows, the
humorist channels close.

In the Privacy of Their Own Condo

He agrees to watch the Woody Allen movie. Usually he hates Woody Allen movies because they're too emotional and loud. But he agrees to watch *Blue Jasmine* because he's sick of the news and the other choice on offer is *Comedy Central*, which is even worse than Woody Allen. *Comedy Central*, he says, is like watching Stephen Leacock on Benzedrine.

They get settled in bed. They'll be watching the bedroom TV. Madeline places the remote on the duvet cover between them.

The movie starts quietly enough – Lorne even chuckles once or twice – but then, little by little, it gets louder, and he starts making snorting sounds. Then he pounds the pillow to re-fluff it, grabs a bedside Kleenex, blows his nose, and asks if she's had enough.

"It's just about over," Madeline says.

They continue watching for another fifteen minutes, reaching the car scene towards the end of the movie, which is a kind of climax. In this scene a man and woman scream at each other at the same time for a full minute while driving in a car.

Lorne can stand it no longer. He flings off the bedcovers and, with his hands over his ears, strides naked into the kitchen.

Madeline turns down the volume on the TV. Soon, Lorne is back in bed, but now his back is turned away from her and the bedcovers are over his head. The water he brought from the kitchen remains untouched on his bedside table.

There are thirteen minutes left in the movie and Madeline wants to see how it ends. She turns down the volume even further so that she's watching the characters' lips.

When the movie is over she reads a little. The room is quiet. Lorne remains turned away from her with the covers still over his head.

When Madeline turns off her bedside lamp, she says, "I liked your naked dash to the kitchen just now. It got me quite excited."

Under the covers, Lorne grins. His head emerges. "You don't say?"

Thirty-Two Years On

The mung beans sat there rotting
while I waited for his explanation.

The Missing Beacon

"Why is there no beacon at the end of the Avenue when there is clearly an ocean there with pleasure boats going by and cargo ships in the channel beyond? Shouldn't they be guided by a beacon?"

This is the question Rhonda Booth, an English teacher at the high school, asked the town's archivist.

She found him at the Municipal Hall in a tiny room at the bottom of some stairs.

"There never was a beacon at the end of the Avenue," the archivist told her. "There was a beacon on a nearby island but it was never lit."

The archivist smiled at Rhonda from behind his cluttered desk. His office had one dirty window, high up.

Like something out of Dickens, Rhonda thought.

The archivist, whose name was Arnold Screech, had been on the job for many years. Hardly anyone had questions for him about the town's history. He was delighted. He asked Rhonda if she knew about the terrible accident that had happened just beyond the dock during the early part of the last century.

Rhonda said she didn't.

"It made all the headlines," Arnold Screech said. "An overloaded ferry capsized and many lives were lost. But four were saved by people from the W̱SÁNEĆ Nation, who were out clamming, and for this they were awarded medals of bravery from the Canadian government."

"Really?" said Rhonda, thinking: He's like Scheherazade, desperate to keep my attention.

"After the accident the pier was built," said Arnold Screech.

"Ah," said Rhonda. She left him cataloguing a pile of spoons on his desk.

The pier had been a town fixture for decades. Recently a small restaurant specializing in clam chowder had opened down the road from it, occupying what had once been the fish store. This was where Rhonda and her husband, Hugh, had had Saturday lunch on several occasions.

Initially they went to the restaurant because it was somewhere different to eat and because they both liked clam chowder, but before long it was because the waitress there was so friendly. Her name was Sandy, a plump woman in her fifties. She seemed to like Rhonda and Hugh and treated them like old friends. They started to look forward to seeing her.

This pleasant lunch experience continued for a while until, for some unknown reason, Sandy's manner towards them changed. She became less and less friendly until, finally, she found fault with how long they were taking to eat their lunch.

"How much longer will you be? There are customers waiting," she demanded loudly near the end of their meal.

They never went back.

Now when anyone asks them about the restaurant, Hugh says, "Steer clear. That place is a disaster. A ferry once sank not far from there and it's like disaster keeps repeating. This time it's the waitress. She's got a fickle heart. You think she loves you but it's a dangerous lie."

The Great Wonder

The French Immersion teacher and the elementary
school principal had been having frequent sex in the
gym storeroom, an occurrence that happened several
years ago. Eventually they were discovered by the janitor,
who reported them to the school board office.

Around the same time, the Board received a call
from the mother of one of the school's grade three
students. The mother complained that her daughter,
returning after school for her gym bag, had seen the
French teacher and the principal having stand-up sex
beside the volleyball netting. Her daughter, she said, had
been traumatized by what she had witnessed.

After the disciplinary hearing several transfers
occurred within the district. The principal was
reassigned to the post of vice-principal of the middle
school, there to perish, we understood, in the special
hell that is adolescent hormones. The French teacher,
however, was promoted to head of the district French
department and given an office at the school board. This
surprised many people, as did the fact that her husband
didn't leave her.

A couple of years later, the janitor, who'd made
the report, was caught by a parent taking pictures of
boys peeing in the school washroom. For this he was
temporarily suspended and ordered to take counselling.

As to the fates of the traumatized grade three
student and her mother, nothing further is known.
But, certainly, the story stands as one of the town's
great wonders.

Our Naomi Frankl

Worldwide, there are many women named
Naomi Frankl.

There's a Naomi Frankl in England who has a court
judgment against her and one in New York City who
is a senior audit associate. There's one who is moving
from LA to Boston but we don't know why, and one in
Winnipeg, Manitoba, who is a famous food critic and
practitioner of tantric yoga.

In South Africa, Naomi Frankl has added an *e* to
her last name and appears as Naomi Frankel. In Israel,
there's a Naomi Frankl who works at a checkpoint,
though we don't know which one.

Locally, Naomi Frankl is known as Naomi Frank and
practises something she calls "prophetic worship dance."
To do this she wears a long white skirt, black sweatshirt,
and white gloves, and twirls slowly around a room, as if
in a trance. The music she uses is like the music you'd
hear at a spa.

Naomi Frank recently danced at the wedding of
Emily Bott and Kevin Almeda. She danced after the
wedding toasts, as part of the entertainment package,
which included an elderly accordionist playing polka
tunes and a group of ten- and eleven-year-olds from the
town's music academy singing hits from cartoon movies.

The wedding's 125 guests were seated at tables
arranged against the walls of the Community Cultural
Centre. Naomi Frank was the last performance. She
danced longer than the arranged-for five minutes. The
music from her Sony portable kept fading out and
then coming back with a crackle. Finally, after sixteen
minutes, she took her bow.

"Excuse the sound," she told the wedding guests.
"Sorry about the quality. Praise God."

Emily Bott's mother, Arlene, leaned over and hissed at her husband, "Who in God's name was responsible for that? Nobody even clapped!"

Ken Bott shrugged and looked away.

"I'll be blamed," Arlene said to the back of his head. "You just wait. I'll be spending the rest of my life begging Emily for forgiveness. You want to know what an unhappy woman looks like? That'll be me for the next thirty years, with no thanks to Naomi Frank."

Bouquets

The woman's sport was catching bridal bouquets. "It's something you have to plan for. You need to be very strategic about where you place yourself," she told her new friend at the Body Barn.

Both women were in a weight-loss program, exercising side by side on stair climbers.

"Plus, of course," she said, "you have to get invited to the weddings. Or work at them, in catering or behind the bar. As an employee I've never been told not to catch a bouquet. But mostly I'm one of the invited guests."

It pleased her that the other woman seemed interested, and she gaily carried on. "I make sure I'm up front when the bouquets are being thrown. A lot of times the bride doesn't know how far the bouquet is going to go. She just turns her back on everyone and tosses it. Some of the bouquets hit a ceiling, or a chandelier. But mostly they land with a thud right behind the bride. I've had many catches where I've had to jump for it. And I've hit little kids by accident. But I've caught twenty-six bouquets since 2002. Hard work pays off."

"That's a lot of bouquets," said the new friend. "I got married in a registry office so I never got to throw my bouquet. It was too little to throw anyway. Actually, it was a wrist corsage. What about you?"

"Not married yet," said the woman. "Still waiting for my boyfriend to propose. It's been, what? Eleven years? I guess that's why I like catching bouquets. Makes me feel romantic. I always give them back though, the bouquets. Otherwise it would be like kidnapping memories."

"Yeah I guess," said the other woman, and then, "Did you hear that? That popping sound in my chest. I get it every time I use the stair climber."

·"My elbow gives me trouble from using the weights," said the bouquet catcher. "Makes you wonder if this working out is worth it."

They were quiet then. Queen was playing on the gym's sound system – "Crazy Little Thing Called Love" – and they got in sync with the music.

Behind them a determined old woman in pink was pulling ten pounds on the rowing machine. For her the wild era of joy had ended.

Thirteen Years with Myrna

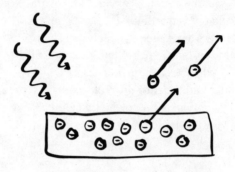

The slamming of car doors.
Tears in the shepherd's pie.

One Alone

"You think odd things while waiting in line at the bank," the young poet was thinking. "Like the way people look timeless when standing naked with wet, stringy hair. It's impossible to tell what century they are in."

The poet was twenty-three years old, out of work, and lately had been sleeping on his mother's couch.

"My life has turned into a sleeper's convention," he thought next. "Everyone in this line, myself included, is like a long-haired goat gnawing at grass in their sleep." He laughed out loud, delighted with the image.

Others in the line gave him censorious looks and he experienced deep misery. Not because of their looks, but because he was now thinking, "In waking life it usually never occurs to us that we are awake." Where had he read that? What did it mean?

A nudge came from behind and he moved two feet forward, experiencing a flutter in his chest, which, he was sure, was not unlike Emily Dickinson's description of hope. Soon he would reach the bank machine, deposit his unemployment cheque, withdraw some cash, and get those boots at Mark's.

"Even clothed," he now thought, "I'm not sure what century I am in." This time he didn't laugh out loud but was happy with the thought nonetheless.

A quote from Thoreau came to his mind: "One alone, still Sunday." The comma, he knew, said everything. Despair overcame him again – if only *he* could say everything.

Outside on the Avenue there was a photograph of the late poet Al Purdy, along with two of his poems. They had been stencilled onto an electrical junction box. It was the town's way of honouring the poet, who had lived there during his final years.

The junction box was on the corner of a busy intersection, in front of a credit union and across from Smitty's Restaurant. Further along the street was the Save-On-Foods parking lot.

One of the Al Purdy poems on the junction box began, "I am learning what a strange lonely place is myself."

The young poet hadn't paid attention to this poem even though it had been on the box for several years and he'd grown up in the town. But all of us here in the bank lineup are hoping that he reads the poem, and soon.

Self-Portrait

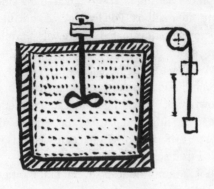

This self-portrait is something Bruno
came up with and I think it's
total genius.

The Happiness Seminar

During a morning walk I stopped to read a flyer for a "Happiness Seminar." It was taped to the side of our community mailbox. The flyer was colourful – pinks and yellows predominated. There was a rainbow, a smiling sun.

"We don't think there's any limit to the time and money and effort you can put into something to create your own happiness," the flyer read. Further details included the time and place of the seminar, though not the cost. Thinking I might have missed this information, I looked more closely.

It was then I noticed several handwritten messages scrawled on various parts of the flyer. One in the right-hand margin said, "There is nowhere to move from happiness. It's a terrible place to be. It's complacency." Beneath this someone had written, "So true."

At the bottom of the flyer the message was in green. It said, "Pleasure is the only thing one should live for. Nothing ages like happiness.—Oscar Wilde."

I thought for a moment about Oscar Wilde's end in that room in France – dejected, unloved, bereft about the wallpaper; "Either it goes or I do," he reportedly said.

A third comment written at the top of the flyer in pencil ended with three angry exclamation marks: "Happy people live. Unhappy people tell others how to live!!!"

So far the comments were 3–0 against the state of happiness. But then I noticed a comment written along the red and yellow bands of the flyer's rainbow that might be construed as pro-happiness. "As long as everyone isn't dead, I'm in."

I pulled out my pen and wrote beside it, "I'm with you!"

And felt good. I was participating with my neighbours in a happiness seminar of our own making. No need to travel anywhere, no need to pay, no need to be anything but anonymous.

I thought of another message about happiness I could add. It was a quote by Samuel Beckett. "Nothing is funnier than unhappiness ... It's the most comical thing in the world."

That'll really add something, I thought, enjoying myself.

I started writing across the smiling sun and got as far as, "Nothing is fun ..." when my pen ran out of ink.

Luckily the street was empty. I walked briskly away from the mailbox.

This Way Out

Anders is the only shoemaker in town. He's thin, dark-haired, about thirty-five or forty.

Since he's the only shoemaker means we have to follow him around. This is because every few months he stops taking customers and closes his shop. Then a while later he'll reopen in a different location. He's been found at the back of the tattoo parlour, on the side of the comic book shop, at the back of the vacuum repair shop.

He's a good shoemaker, not too expensive, and finishes the repairs on time. Usually he smells like marijuana.

When he set up at Nicole's Vintage Clothing, he had a display of pen-and-ink drawings that he'd done. They were on the floor propped against the counter and when I was picking up my clogs – he'd patched a hole in the toe – I bought one for my husband's birthday.

Months later at his next shop, which was located in a side room at the cat rescue place, I told him how much my husband had liked the picture. It was of a partially opened door with a sign above it that read, "This Way Out."

But Anders said he didn't remember drawing the picture. In fact, he said, he didn't remember displaying the pictures at all, and he especially didn't remember selling me one. I'd given him forty dollars for it.

After we had this conversation he paused for a moment. Then he grinned and said, "This is the perfect bookend to the last eight years of my life."

When I heard this it was like a shooting star went across the landscape.

The Merry Cemetery

Young entrepreneurs in Săpânţa, northern Romania have created a graveyard that makes people happy. It's called the Merry Cemetery and has become, say the owners, one of the country's top tourist attractions.

The cemetery practises something called "grave art." Various artists have been commissioned to illustrate headstones and crosses but, unlike the usual biblical or factual information that go with these things, grave markers in the Merry Cemetery showcase a person's personality flaws or their imagined last words.

A forty-two-year-old man, who was run over by a subway car, has this written on his gravestone: "I enjoyed life so much, I went to Western Europe; may it be cursed along with the Paris Metro."

Another man, who died in a freak truck accident, has written on his headstone: "The truck rolled over and I was smothered. This is no way to die." The headstone features a carving of a truck with two feet sticking out from beneath it.

The inscription for a woman, aged sixty-three, who owned several nail salons, reads, "I was wealthy and kept it all for myself. Now I am dead and have nothing."

"The Merry Cemetery is not just a cemetery," says sculptor Jerzy Pinca, who crafted many of the headstones. "The idea was to create a cemetery filled with modern morality tales, ones that make people laugh at death."

Rumour has it that those behind Count Dracula, Romania's leading tourist brand, are worried about this rival attraction. Will dark humour trump legend and bloodlust, people wonder?

Says crucifix carver and cemetery co-owner, Cezara Toth, "There is nothing funny about Count Dracula, is there? A figure based on Vlad the Terrible. He butchered his family in the 1500s, including cousins and aunts, including his favourite son and even his grandmother. These days people are in the mood for some non-political entertainment. They want something lighthearted and fun. That's what they get at the Merry Cemetery."

Waiting Room

The young man wearing a black suit, white shirt, and black scarf sat beside his grandfather in Dr. Burns's waiting room. Dr. Burns was one of the few GPs in town.

"I've brought my own undertaker," the old man told the other waiting patients.

The skinny girl with the pink hair laughed. She was wearing a net skirt and silver shoes.

"I used to play the accordion at dances and weddings," the old man said loudly. "But the ones who care about the polka are old and not dancing anymore. I was playing to empty floors."

"Granddad."

"What? It's the truth!"

The grandson looked away.

"Furthermore," the old man said, "the world is run by thugs. It would be nice for a change if they saved people instead of killing them."

"Granddad."

"I'll bet you'd like to know how I dye my hair," the pink-haired girl said to the old man. She didn't wait for a reply. "It's trial and error to get the right shade. Somewhere between baby pink and hot pink. You couldn't buy this shade in a bottle. You have to play with the mixes yourself. Not everyone can get these results."

"What?" said the old man.

The girl raised her voice. "I said, not everyone gets the results I get. My friend, Amber," she continued, "dyes one half of her hair pink and the other blue, which looks all right when she wears pigtails but not so good otherwise."

She went on to say that her social work practicum was going to be at the food bank. She was proud that she'd received the placement looking the way she did but concluded that one look at her would cause people to be happy and that can't be a bad thing, can it?

By now many of the waiting patients were smiling. But not the old man.

He turned to his grandson. "I'm too old for this," he said. "Who do I have to sleep with to get out of here?"

Worn Rug

His wife had already established what was going on
in the home. Because of her, things had been running
smoothly for years: every drawer and cupboard had a
reason; every sheet had a reunion with the washing
machine on Sunday.

But when you're newly retired, as Dan was, and
home full-time, you're disrupting all that. You can say,
"I'll set the rules now," but it's a waste of breath. The
cement has been dry for years.

"There's no point whining about things," Donna
said. "Find an interest."

Donna's interest was people. People made her happy.

"I love people," she said. "I'd love to squeeze every
darn last one of them."

To remember the many people she loved, she
likened them to an animal or a bird or a flower,
summing up a person, for example, as "a sweet little
wren" or "a tuberous begonia."

Others, still, she likened to furniture. Gordon,
across the street, was "like the design of a Chinese
lantern." Which was true, according to Dan; there
was something secretive about Gordon. Nikki, around
the corner, was "a sixties-style armchair." And Chad,
down the road, was a "contemporary table with an
unusual shape."

About Dan in retirement, Donna declared, "You're a
worn rug but still pretty bright!"

This pleased Dan. It meant that his colour would be
slow to fade.

The tuberous begonia was Jenny Weeks, a widow,
who lived in a rancher on the next block over. She was
a person, in Dan's estimation, who lived up to her

moniker, managing to be both fleshy and delicate at the same time. And the best part, Dan was happy to note, was that her door was always open.

Study of Contrasts

He (R) orders beer.
She (L) orders one tablespoon of Scotch over ice.

The Flight of Brown Owl

Brown Owl ran off with the tai chi master. Left her
husband of twenty-eight years, two kids, one grandson,
and ran off to Puerto Rico. A month before this
happened we saw Brown Owl and the tai chi master
necking in the Save-On parking lot on a busy Saturday
afternoon. It was summer. We thought the tai chi master
must be a Latino dancer because of the way he moved,
which was fluid and slow-dancing and dominant. We
didn't see his face that day, just his poncho-covered
back embracing Brown Owl. We got a good look at
her, though. She had on a low-necked sleeveless top,
and her head was thrust back, and between kisses she
was laughing.

Fifteen years earlier Brown Owl had been our
daughter's Brownie leader. That's why, until we got to
know her, we always referred to her as Brown Owl. She
taught Teddy how to make a fire out of paraffin and
twigs, and how to sew on buttons, and also the Brownie
Promise, which is:

> *I Promise to do my best,*
> *To be true to myself, my beliefs and Canada.*
> *I will take action for a better world*
> *And respect the Brownie Law.*

This law concerned being honest and taking care of the
world, not a bad law to abide by.

As it turned out, we were wrong about the tai chi
master being Latino. He was as British as an old biscuit,
and named Philip. And he wasn't much to look at – a
man in his fifties, small in stature, with thin, sandy-
coloured hair and pale skin. For someone who'd dazzled
with his hot moves in the Save-On parking lot he was,

most of the time, reserved. We decided that this reserve was a British form of tai chi serenity.

They stayed here on two occasions. Brown Owl – Melinda – was a friend of Jeff's, our tenant who lived in the downstairs suite. So we were a second-hand party to the story.

Jeff and Melinda had taken a tai chi class from Philip, who was visiting from England. This is how Melinda and Philip met. They had fallen instantly, Jeff said, in love. Or, as Jeff further told us, "The dragon sighs and the tiger roars." Meaning, as he explained to our uncomprehending faces, that Melinda and Philip were a powerful yin and yang situation; their union was inevitable.

In any event, the romance went from a spark to a bonfire within days. Melinda left her husband, who had a roofing business, and began staying with Philip at the Travelodge motel on the Avenue. But that got expensive, so they stayed here for three weeks in Jeff's suite, while they got organized for their flight to Puerto Rico. Jeff gave them the bedroom; he took the pullout in the suite's living room.

Jeff had lived in the suite for five years by then. He was a gentle man in his early forties who tended his elderly parents a few streets over. They paid him enough to live on, so he didn't need to work. He set out bird feeders around the suite – he could identify all the songbirds – and grew succulents and, inside, orchids, often inviting us in to look at a new bloom. There was a small cement Buddha he'd placed in the flower bed beneath the suite's windows and we'd notice him now and then sitting cross-legged before it and meditating. Occasionally, he had a woman down there, one we called

Spanky because he told us she liked to be spanked. But we didn't hear any of this because his ceiling is insulated.

Melinda and Philip left for Puerto Rico at the end of that summer. Philip had a seasonal job at a resort there, offering tai chi classes to people on vacation. Then several months later Jeff told us that Melinda was back because she'd been deported. Her visa had expired but she'd tried to stay on anyway. She returned to our town, leaving Philip behind at his job.

There was a happy ending, though.

She house-sat in the area for a few months and then stayed here for two weeks with Jeff while she got her papers in order. Then Philip came and got her. By then it was summer again.

The last time we saw her she was striding arm in arm with Philip along the Avenue. It was a hot, bright afternoon in late August, the day they were scheduled to catch a late flight to Vancouver, and then to Puerto Rico. She wore a green silk scarf around her neck; it flowed behind her and caught the light brilliantly. Her long, red hair bounced on her shoulders as she walked. There was an ecstatic look on her face but whether this was caused by the happiness of finding her master, her man, or her freedom, or all three, we had no way of knowing.

Hero

Eli may look like he's absorbed elsewhere – sitting on the front porch, cleaning his face with his paw – but he's not. He's watching the bushes at the side of the house. This is where Scout, the next-door neighbour's rescue dog, a chow mix, emerged so suddenly last April.

At the time, Jeremy was in the sandbox with his toys.

A prolonged rustling in the bushes alerted Eli. When Scout pushed through, he immediately sighted his prey and ran. He was going to hurl himself at Jeremy.

Jeremy's mother was hanging the wash and was too far away to help. But Eli sprang, leaping onto the dog's back as he was about to strike. Then he held on and rode the terrified dog to the end of the driveway. Scout howling, his neck bloodied from Eli's claws.

Now the town has decided that a cat this brave should be awarded the Hero Dog Award. There'll be a special ceremony at the band shell on Canada Day. Eli, together with the saved baby and the baby's parents, will receive the town's warm applause.

By then Scout will have been euthanized and his owners shamed.

"We are not afraid to lose an animal," say Eli's owners – "or, even, a previously good neighbour – if it works for the story."

Perspective

Gary and his ancient mother, Ruth, decide that the fierce-looking young people with black lips and rings through their noses, who are blocking their way into the TD Bank on this lovely June afternoon, are really clowns sent by the universe to delight them.

The Acting Mayor

The acting mayor once threw a jar of French's mustard at our front door. This was when he was in grade eight and my husband was the counsellor at his school and responsible for the rowdy kids. The acting mayor had been disciplined for some reason and, as my husband explained, was "acting out," getting revenge for whatever punishment he'd received.

It was a Friday night and we were having dinner with friends. We heard the jar hit the door and the dog bark. When we went to investigate we saw the acting mayor and his pal Shawn running down the driveway. Mustard dripped down the door and the area beside the door and our friends didn't know whether to be aghast or amused. My husband assured us that though the boy was a goofball, he was basically a good kid and wouldn't do anything really harmful. After the guests left he cleaned up the mess.

Now the boy is thirty-five years old and a member of the municipal council. It's hard for us to understand how this happened, to fathom the change in him from a thrower of mustard to a representative of the community.

This month he's taking his turn as acting mayor. His picture was in the local paper showing him at a tree-planting ceremony. He still looks like he did in grade eight, beefy and round-faced, though now he's spoken of as a hard worker and a model citizen, with not one mention of his former goofiness.

Besides being on Council, he has a local gardening business and, as it turns out, has begun cutting our lawn. Not him personally but his employee, Mason, who previously cut our lawn for four years and was recently hired on.

The first email invoice we received from the acting mayor's business included a message that said, "Greetings from your Garden Professional." The email was addressed to my husband's proper name, "Mr. Ash," and not to "Mr. Ashhole," which is what my husband was called by students those many years ago.

Bobby

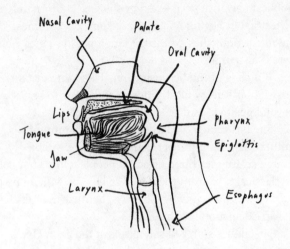

They brought Bobby in because they needed a glamour guy in the cave.

The Gift

Ginni Track plans to celebrate her fiftieth birthday by conducting volunteer musicians and singers in a scaled-down version of Mendelssohn's *Elijah*, an oratorio with a biblical narrative performed by soloists, chorus, and orchestra, but having no action, scenery, or costumes. The music embodies a sense of longing and sadness, but there is also uplift.

Which is fitting because Ginni Track, an amateur musician, is said by her friends in real estate to be "beyond positive" and "a lover of life."

She has rented the large hall at the Community Cultural Centre for the performance. There will be enough seating for three hundred people to hear her play the classical tuba from the raised stage. She will not be deterred from conducting, she says, because the tuba has a low participation level in *Elijah*.

Jarrod, her son, will sell tickets at the door. Her daughter, Brittney, will act as usher, and, Larry, her father and biggest cheerleader, will be filming the evening from his scooter using a rented camcorder.

"To be the centre of the universe for just one evening is a true honour," Ginni Track has said. "This will be my birthday gift to myself."

Her Cake

On her fourteenth birthday Eileen McCue was sitting
at the kitchen table with her mother and said, "Today
I am fourteen years old but when I'm eighteen I'll
be gone away."

This happened years ago in Scotland.

"How do you know?" said her mother.

"I know. I can feel it," said Eileen.

Her mother said, "You'll change your mind."

Eileen, however, didn't change her mind. When she
turned eighteen she said to her mother, "This is it. I'm
leaving for Canada next week."

Her mother said, "Over my dead body."

Eileen said back, "If you have to be dead I promise
to bury you."

No one went to the train station to see Eileen off.
But at the last moment her mother appeared. She said,
"You forgot your umbrella."

Eileen never saw her mother again.

This is the story Eileen told Shannon Armstrong,
the young reporter for the local paper; she was writing
a piece about Eileen's birthday. For the interview Eileen
had been moved by staff to the Sun Room.

To sum up, Shannon had been told by her editor to
ask the question, "What's your secret for living so long?"

"Everyone loves to read about that," he said.

Eileen answered the question. "I got to be one
hundred and two years old because I followed my own
road," she said. "My advice to anybody is this: If you
think, 'That's the road I'm going to take,' take it. You'll
be happy for the rest of your life."

"But what about food?" Shannon asked. "Was
there something special you ate that caused you to live
past a hundred?"

"I drank," said Eileen. "Two glasses of Scotch every day. Sometimes three."

"And your family?"

"Never saw the need."

"No husband? Children?"

"No."

Shannon took her picture.

Back at the office she worked on the write-up. She asked the editor if she should mention the Scotch and the part about Eileen not having a family. She was new at the job, just three months out of university.

The editor said, "It's supposed to be a light piece." He paused. "I think we'll scrap this one and put a caption beneath her picture instead. Write something like, 'Resident Eileen McCue celebrates her 102nd birthday at the Seaside Care Home.'"

Shannon looked disappointed.

"Okay, write a few words about her coming from Scotland, whenever it was. And how long she's been in the home. Say she liked her birthday cake."

Shannon still looked disappointed.

"Okay," said the editor, "we'll put it on the front page."

Happy New Year

The Christian roofer had been phoning us for six years. He had some hope, it seemed, that we would ask him to replace our roof. He phoned every three or four months. One year he phoned on New Year's Eve.

"Hello," he said in the slight Eastern European accent we'd become accustomed to. "George here. Would you be thinking of replacing your roof in the coming year?"

It was 10:30 p.m. *The Rocky Horror Picture Show* video had ended and we were hanging around the kitchen, counting down the minutes to midnight. We'd watched the kettle boil and were sharing a tea bag: two cups, one bag.

"Not right now," my husband said. "I'm sorry, but we don't need a new roof."

We were pleasant to George because he was always pleasant to us. "Did he say Happy New Year?" I asked with some anxiety. It had been a lonely New Year's Eve: the video, the tea bag. No, he hadn't.

The way we discovered that George was a Christian happened during a call in which my husband, as usual, had turned him down. Then George tried a new tactic, suggesting that we call *him* when we needed a new roof. "But don't call on a Tuesday evening," he said, "that's Bible study night."

The fact that George was a Christian interested us: we wondered how far his faith in one day replacing our roof would go. And because we're not Christians per se, preferring as much as possible to dwell in transience, we wondered what effect his faith might have on us over time. Would the three of us grow old together while our roof grew over with moss? Would we continue to gently tell him, "No, thank you, not this year"?

George's idea of us contacting *him* about the roof was short-lived. Before long, his intermittent calls resumed. "What is it," we asked each other, "that causes George to believe so surely that he will one day replace our roof? And how did we acquire this random person in our lives so that now his calls have become like calls from a long-ago friend, both dreaded and desired?"

Then, after six years, a new thought startled us. The reason that George was phoning about our roof all the time was because this was his job in life – he is a roofer – and to get jobs he calls people up. He didn't have a personal relationship with us at all, and he wasn't calling to felicitate meditations on the nature of our lives or, even, to imbue us with Christian beliefs.

When we thought this thought we felt bad. Bad for having so blithely and self-centredly missed the obvious. Bad that for six years we may have strung along an honest, hard-working man. A decent person. We felt especially mean to have done this. Further, we felt that such meanness of spirit may have contributed to our succession of lonely New Year's Eves, and to our transient existence being, we had to admit, a state less than fulsome.

So on a Saturday morning in late November, and after six years, my husband called him up. "Now is the time, George," he said.

George didn't sound surprised or overjoyed to hear from us. He merely said in his usual calm way that he'd arrive at our house that afternoon between the hours of two and four.

When we saw him in person we felt cheered. He looked exactly as we'd imagined he would: small, fair-skinned, mid-sixties, wearing beige work clothes and a baseball cap. His truck was new and very clean, as we'd known it would be.

George nodded to us as he climbed his aluminum ladder to the roof to look things over. From the driveway below we watched him poking at the shingles. A while later we heard him whistling "Rock of Ages."

When we asked him how he was getting on he called down, shaking his head sadly. "You'll need a complete roof replacement." He stood on our roof in quiet triumph. "There's moss on the shingles," he told us. "There's terrible rot within."

By then we couldn't agree more. For the first time in six years we felt as if a load was about to be lifted from our shoulders. The terrible rot within was about to be removed.

It was a bright day and the sun glinted off George's glasses as he descended each rung of the ladder. Right there in the driveway, as George drove away with the promise of a new roof before Christmas, we began planning a crowded New Year's Eve party – loud, boozy, sinful.

Middle C

We've decided that by staying in the middle
we'll be least bothered by the pillars of
doubt that line much of the journey.
We can focus on ourselves and our questions.
Such as, Why is Anne's character inspired
by Casey? Why is some of the dynamic
between her and Ken so tense?

The Era of Hating the Accordion Has Arrived

The young man said he had strong opinions about the accordion because he grew up with the instrument. His grandfather had played it at weddings and dances, and as a boy he was made to go along and watch.

"Old people," he told the youth court judge, "would be jumping about, sort of dancing together. And there was shouting all the time because people kept banging into each other. Women were always screaming. And drunk women would try to get me to dance with them. They had big red lips and sweating faces and they smelled."

Meanwhile, he said, "Granddad would be in another dimension, playing one disgusting tune after another, and ignoring me completely."

Even worse, he said, was during the intermission when he'd be given money for chips and a pop. There was always this fat guy at the concession stand trying to feel him up.

"It was horrible," he said.

He still felt traumatized.

"Thank you, Myron," said the judge. "Is there anything else you'd like to say before we finish up here?"

Myron said, "Only that the accordion world has done a bad job of promoting itself. When you go to an accordion event they are playing polkas. They are feeding into the stereotype, which is old people playing dumb music. My grandfather still does events, but nobody dances when he plays anymore. They just sit there and wait for him to finish."

"You understand," the judge interrupted, "that you've been accused of smashing the front window of Madrona Music Supply and damaging the two accordions on display there?"

"Yes, I do," said Myron. "But do you even know what a beginning accordion player sounds like? Like ten fifty-foot chainsaws attached to flaming rotor blades in the middle of a railroad destruction derby!"

"You're an interesting fellow, Myron," the judge said kindly. "In your black suit and tie. You look like you work in a funeral home. Not like a common criminal."

"I'm not a criminal," said Myron. "It's just – can't you see? Accordions don't belong in the world anymore."

Solace

"I've spent a lot of time doing angry," the young woman told the intake worker at Community Services. "I mean, my mother was angry. My grandfather was angry. Cody, the family dog was an angry dog, didn't like anything. The birds screaming outside the kitchen window were angry. Seagulls, crows. They drove me nuts. My father was angry. My baby sister was angry, never stopped crying. Every teacher I've ever had was angry. Every cat was a mean cat. I've been around anger all my life."

The woman leaned forward in her chair. "Is it any wonder I'm happy with this little Prozac pill?

The Man in Question

People in the town began sharing a few of the known facts about the man in question.

It was said he'd been a commercial airline pilot and was lately retired. That there'd been an early marriage that ended in divorce, no children, and that he'd travelled frequently across the country to visit his ailing mother, who was in a care home; when she died he took her death badly.

It was also known that during the winter he vacationed in New Zealand, hired a car, and spent three months driving around and staying in hotels. It was said he was on antidepressants.

A few years ago he'd had a relationship with a middle-aged woman named Tina – people referred to her as "The Hat" because she always wore a white hat of some kind, winter or summer. It was said the relationship with Tina didn't end well, that the man found her too much to handle.

It appeared, as well, that he didn't have any close friends, only other pilots, retired or not, whom he'd meet in local bars – the meetings casual, the bars frequented on a rotating basis. His talk there consisted mostly of details about his collection of vintage cars. He spent considerable sums of money on their restoration: a dune buggy, an Austin-Healey convertible painted British racing green, a pink and white 1957 Chevrolet Bel Air.

The man owned a large house a mile from town and had a house cleaner and a gardener. In the spring he'd been seen out walking. On each sighting he was wearing an orange down jacket, a toque, and wool mittens no matter what the weather, and there'd been some hot days. He walked the same route twice each day – down the length of the Avenue, then back again. He'd nod hello in passing, people said, but never stop to talk.

He was short, his face swollen-looking, flushed. It was said he had trouble with his feet, possibly chilblains. It was said he was bored, that he'd been drinking heavily.

It was in the Chevrolet Bel Air that he died of carbon monoxide poisoning after closing the garage door and leaving the engine running. He was found three days later by a neighbour. He was sixty-eight years old. It was said he'd planned his suicide because the week before he'd fired the house cleaner and the gardener. It is not known if he had a will or if he left a final message. It is not known how his body was disposed of. There was no funeral.

An impromptu gathering was held three weeks later at one of the pubs he frequented. It was attended mainly by men he drank with. Tina was there with an elderly man from Palm Springs, said to be her latest boyfriend. She was wearing a white dress and a white straw hat. She was heard to remark that even this happy town was not immune from sadness.

At the gathering, someone stood and spoke of the man as an excellent pilot and a devoted son. There was a toast in which his name was mentioned; the toaster wished that he rest in peace.

Because it was summer the outside patio was open. His drinking companions had pooled their money to provide a cheese platter, a vegetable tray, and a tray of chicken wings for those attending. There was a cash bar. Someone was heard to say that the man in question was not one of those guys you have to drag off the stage.

It wasn't exactly laughter that erupted as a result of the comment, more like a shared grimace. Still, the words provided some relief.

Are You Are Who?

They'd been told that the transition from working life to retirement could be a difficult one, but they hadn't anticipated the sense of aimlessness they were now experiencing.

At dinner Diane said, "We no longer seem to get any momentum going. It's like we've become a pair of old trucks rusting on blocks."

"We've become idle," said Jim. "Like that old guy in the café, the one in the blue windbreaker who's always sitting alone. Did you see the boxed pie he had on his lap this morning?"

"Yes, I did. I hope he's really a Joseph Cornell figure."

The American artist Joseph Cornell was a recent interest of Diane's. She said, "Cornell also had crumbs on the front of his jacket. And he'd spend hours alone in cafés with a cup of coffee and a piece of soft cake. But then he'd go home with all the bits and pieces he found in junk stores and create those amazing boxes."

"Maybe the guy in the café does that," said Jim. "Maybe he's got a basement full of boxes."

"And that box on his lap this morning," said Diane, "might really contain a black comb, a lottery ticket, and a grocery list he found on the sidewalk!"

"Slow down," said Jim. "The box might only contain an apple pie."

"And that is so sad," said Diane. "Do you think he's going to eat it by himself?"

"Why not?" said Jim. "Cut into eighths it could last a week."

"My father could make a stew last a week."

"Your father's been dead for thirty-six years," said Jim.

"What's that got to do with it? He could still make a stew last a week."

"And a razor blade last a month," said Jim. "If I hear one more of your father's virtues I'm going to get really tired."

"That hurts," said Diane.

"Well? You're always bringing him up."

"Just fuck off," said Diane. "Just really fuck off and stay there."

There was silence for a few minutes, and then Jim said, "Have it your way. But before I fuck off why don't we have a little drinky. Some of that Macallan's I've been saving. Then we could walk to the pier. Catch the sunset."

"Okay," said Diane. "But only if you promise not to disparage my father."

"A saint if ever there was one."

"I mean it."

"I promise."

"A walk sounds nice. Maybe after we could stop for a drink at the Flying Mermaid."

"Why not?" said Jim.

"I'll just go brush my teeth," said Diane.

Happy Hour

Leanne Rhodes was sitting at the hotel bar talking to her friend Bonnie, who was the bartender there. It was Happy Hour. Leanne was on her third beer.

After listening to Leanne's story, Bonnie said, "Yeah well. Tell them thanks for the invite but no thanks. You won't be bringing your nine-year-old kid to the all-male strip show, even if it is a fundraiser for the food bank. Leave some jars of spaghetti sauce or something outside the Centre door instead."

Leanne said something.

"Okay," said Bonnie, "don't leave anything. But if you take Bella it'll be a quiet ride home in the car. Believe me, I've been there. Bella won't be talking. You'll feel like shit."

Leanne didn't say anything.

Old Raymond, a regular, shouted in their direction from a stool at the other end of the bar. "When I win the lottery I'll buy a Learjet and travel around," he said. "I'll need the jet for my dogs so they won't be left behind. I'll say toodle-loo to the dump I'm living in and visit friends back east."

"Good for you," said Bonnie, and returned to Leanne. "Picture the scene," she said. "It'll be raining hard. The car radio won't be working, or the heater. You won't be pulling into McDonald's for a snack because Bella won't be giving you the time of day. There'll just be this crazy woman – you – with a cigarette hanging off her lip and whining at her daughter, 'It was supposed to be a comedy show. I honestly didn't know.'"

Leanne laughed.

Raymond called out again. "Everyone will benefit. I'll fly to Del Mar for the races. I'll take in the Kentucky Derby. I'll hire a full-time vet for the dogs, drink hundred-dollar bottles of Scotch. Have salmon every fucking night. Eat cake for breakfast." He ran out of breath and began coughing.

Bonnie ignored him. "Use your head," she said to Leanne. "Bella's grades aren't going to get better because you took her to a strip show. She won't suddenly start thinking you're the greatest mom in the world. They don't think that till they're over thirty. If ever."

Leanne said something.

"Yeah well," said Bonnie. "I had that kind of mother too. It's no excuse."

Raymond shouted, "And if there's anything you're wanting, just ask and you got it. I'll be looking good sitting on my pile of bucks."

Aria

Two high-school grads in formal gowns – one in pink taffeta, one in green satin – rushed into Shoppers Drug Mart on the morning of the promenade, which was scheduled to begin at Memorial Park at eleven, fifteen minutes away. The park was where graduating students in their gowns and tuxes would mingle with teachers, family, and other grads before moving on to the graduation ceremony in the school gym. It was a years-long tradition.

A white stretch limousine with its engine running waited for the girls outside the drugstore. The park was four blocks away.

The girls were soon in the checkout line with their purchases – perfume, hand wipes, long-lash mascara. They seemed to exist in another dimension. They were larger than anyone else in the store. Their hair was piled high, their bosoms operatic. Each moment promised an aria.

A woman ahead of them, who had a baby and a cart filled with packs of diapers, told them to take her place in line.

The girls effused gratitude. Then they were gone. People watched them drive off.

An older woman in line said, "They're like royalty, aren't they? Like princesses."

The woman with the baby looked glum. "That was me three years ago."

The young cashier in her beige uniform sighed, "That was me last year."

The older employee bagging beside her said, "That was me thirty years ago!"

No one laughed. People resettled in line.

The first to speak again was the young cashier
to the woman with the baby. "That'll be $31.68. Visa,
cash, or debit?"

I was there, at the back of the line with three
birthday cards and a bottle of vitamin B12. I wanted to
speak up and quote a line from a James Tate poem to
put things into perspective. The line was from "Mob
of Good Old Boys" and ended with, "Life is fragile and
as beautiful as a spider's web and the wind is blowing,
always blowing."

But thought the better of it. I sensed that no
one would be interested in the poem just then. Only
in whether or not the rain would hold off for the
grad promenade.

The Great Delight

There were eleven women taking a weekend-long workshop called "Freeing Your Art." It was held in the instructor's home studio.

The instructor, an artist himself, was a grey-haired man in his late fifties. The students were middle-aged and older.

Saturday morning was spent copying a still life – a bowl of green grapes, a jug – after which a lunch of squash soup and homemade bread was served by the instructor's wife.

When lunch was over the instructor announced that the exciting part of the workshop would now begin. Each student would be posing in the nude, he said. Not in front of each other, in front of him. He'd be taking their pictures in a small room off the studio and from these pictures each student would create her masterpiece. One by one during the afternoon, he said, they'd be summoned for the photo session. While this was happening the other students would continue working on their canvasses.

"An artist cannot be free in her art until she frees herself from inhibitions," the instructor said. His job was to help each student do this.

There was some tittering amongst the students, but no one declined to have their picture taken. Hadn't they signed up to be freed?

One after another they were called to the room and told to disrobe behind the Chinese screen in the corner. Then they were directed to lie across a divan, which was placed in front of the instructor's tripod. The divan was covered with a blue silk spread. The poses, the instructor told them, could be as demure or explicit as they wished.

Several props were provided – hats, large feathers, artificial roses, colourful ribbons.

The instructor took several pictures of each woman, transferring copies to their cellphones soon after, telling them to paint one of the pictures he had sent, adding that these paintings, under his guidance, should be "filled with light." They were to start work on the self-portraits immediately and to work on them at his studio the following day.

Each self-portrait canvas was three by five feet, the cost of which was included in the cost of the weekend workshop (325 dollars), although the paints were not.

The really exciting thing, the instructor later told the group, was that their finished paintings would be included in his upcoming show at the Community Cultural Centre, a month away. This caused sounds of great delight to erupt amongst the students.

Finally, the afternoon of the show arrived. The nude self-portraits were hung in a back corner of the room. The instructor's large collection, as was his due, hung front and centre. His were lively paintings, each one in bright reds, yellows, and blues, and each of a single ballerina. To set the mood, music from *Swan Lake* was piped in through the Centre's sound system.

While the people who viewed the students' work might have been shocked or embarrassed to see the semi-pornographic poses of women they knew, either personally or by sight – bridge players, grandmothers, a bank teller, the receptionist in the orthodontist's office – the comment book at the entrance to the show didn't reflect this feeling. "Nice colours" and "Very interesting" were the most frequent phrases used.

As for the students themselves, one woman announced to a viewer that the painting of herself with a red rose in her mouth and a come-hither look in her eyes was going to be hung above her bed – at her husband's insistence.

Noticeable, though, was the air of defiance that many of the students now possessed, as if to say, "We're artists now. We've been validated. We're free."

Also noticeable was the affable instructor holding forth at the sale table, signing up women for his next workshop.

Law of Roundness

First principle: You don't have to
be young and beautiful and thin
to have good things happen to you.

The Great Happiness

Most days you see him pushing his walker along the Avenue. Or sitting beside the bronze statue of the fisherman that's attached to the bench on the south side of the street.

His name is Brian Marr and he has a long white braid that sticks out the back of his ball cap, a feature that gives him an attractive bohemian look. He lives alone in subsidized housing and claims he spends only ten dollars a week for food, mainly for the ingredients to make pea soup and to have a little chocolate as a treat.

Once he did art on the side while working in an Avenue bookstore that specializes in used poetry and fiction titles.

During that time a poet from Calgary came to town to give a reading at the Red Brick Café. She browsed the bookstore where Brian Marr was working and was taken with one of the shadow boxes he had on display there. Much to his delight she arranged to buy it. Inside the chosen box was a sunlit scene from the Avenue – a man walking a dog, a woman pushing a stroller.

Though this was the only time he sold one of his creations, Brian says that the experience – packing and shipping the box to Calgary, the correspondence with the poet, the two-hundred-dollar payment – was "magnificent." He says the afterglow from that great happiness is still with him.

2

Good Times

"Stars don't cost that much," my mother-in-law once
said. "One hundred, two hundred, five hundred dollars.
Some include planets."

She bought herself a small one near the Big Dipper
and named it Irene, after herself.

Somewhere there's a proof of purchase ticket from
the Own-A-Star Foundation.

Irene would point at the sky after a few
drinks. "That star is mine," she'd say, "the dinky
pinky-blue one."

She liked a good time and would ask the dog during
Saturday night cards, "Well, what do you think of the
weekend so far?"

We had her cremated in her full-length mink coat.
That was something a woman had to have in the 1950s
and early '60s – a mink coat. That and a Cadillac car and
a pair of diamond earrings.

When the time came there was no Cadillac and we
found only one diamond earring, a stud. My husband
wore it until the dog came into the story again and the
earring disappeared off the bedside table.

We searched the boulevard for days but all we found
was dirt and twigs and diamond-free poop.

Let it be said that our generation also likes a good
time – we have an appreciation for loud music and
easy laughs. We have our own stars, too, mainly the
cerebral kind.

When the time comes they'll cremate us with our
drugs, our bamboo flutes.

Law of Now

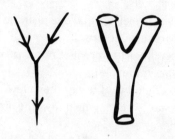

It's like a bell rings in their heads, telling them to come here and wait.

Seasonal Wonderment

The world is incredibly self-obsessed, the woman was thinking. She was sipping an eggnog latte, the café's Christmas special.

And it's not just celebrities, she thought, it's everyone, myself included. Everyone is wanting an audience. Women are lifting up their shirts and posting their stretch marks on Facebook. People are falling out of stopped taxis half-naked. She'd heard it happens all the time. Then someone takes a picture and thousands of people get an online glimpse of a bare bum hitting the pavement.

She was thinking about this when she read – or misread – a headline in one of the café's tabloids: "Fly Swallows Nicole Kidman." She went on to imagine the story: it happened on a film set in Australia during the first week of December; one moment Nicole Kidman was shielding her eyes from the outback sun and the next moment she was gone; a production assistant named Lisa saw it happen; flies in Australia are not only carnivorous, they're fast.

Now here's a cause for seasonal wonderment, the woman thought. On a movie screen Nicole Kidman would be fifteen feet tall but inside a fly she'd be what? A sixteenth of an inch? Microscopic?

Hardly there at all, the woman decided. And no one alongside to take that Merry Christmas video.

The Special Thing

I'd been off in the corner with my chin on my lap. There was dust on my shoes. So I took some online quizzes to cheer myself up.

Right away there was good news. The sandwich quiz said I'm a grilled cheese, an answer I liked because it confirmed my sense of self – crisp on the outside, soft on the inside.

On the next quiz, "Which Classic Author Is Your Soulmate?," I got the sunny sex god Henry Miller, which was so-so. I'd read *Tropic of Cancer* in bed with a flashlight when I was twelve, and all I remember is one sentence: "Her nipples were as hard as diamonds." This description has annoyed me for years.

I redid the quiz and got George Santayana.

Nothing ages you like George Santayana.

On the "Who Is Your Animal Soulmate?" quiz I got a dog. I liked that. The quiz said, "You want to lie on your back and have someone rub your belly, tell you you're the special thing."

Other quizzes were predictable. For a city I was Paris; for a bird, a crow; for my dream job, a firefighter; for a Shakespearean character, Ophelia; for a colour, puce, a word that means the colour of dried blood when a flea is squished. I looked it up. It's French.

"Discover Your True Personality!" caught me off guard. After my answers were tallied, it said, "You are cynical and negative and nobody likes being around you."

I redid the quiz, reversing my previous answers. It said, "You are cynical and negative and nobody likes being around you."

I redid the quiz a third time and got the same answer.

Moving on, I found a quiz that would reveal my true dog personality, the result being, "You are a Pomeranian, fluffy and cute and smart."

This pleased me. You can't buy a personality like that.

Clouds, Glen

It's quite difficult seeing people decide what they felt was important in your life, what you were all about, Jean W. Lynch was thinking as she "sat in" on the obituary-writing session her husband Marty had convened for family and friends. She was an experimental novelist and had recently died.

"Jean W. was like a bird you can't catch, going here, going there with her thinking," Marty was saying.

"That's right," said Jean W.'s brother, Bob. "It was hard to keep up. I always wondered where she got that from. Mom and Dad never went anywhere. In their minds, I mean."

"She loved history, if that counts," said Hope, Bob's wife. "She loved to disappear into TV costume dramas."

"I shouldn't say this but I couldn't make any sense of her books," said Jean W.'s cousin, Maureen. "You had to wonder what was going on in her head."

"Her books," said Jean W.'s best friend, Hester, "were like an offering of Zen-like experiences in the midst of a chaotic world."

"What does that mean?" said Maureen.

"She tried to look at things with fresh eyes."

"I still don't get it."

"Well, she was messy, painful, and beautiful, that I do know," said Marty, in Jean W.'s defence.

"I always believed in her as a human," said Judy, Jean W.'s spin instructor.

"She researched her options before she went, you know," said Marty.

"Did she? That was brave," said Hope.

"She took the up-elevator to Heaven. Don't ask me how she arranged it. But she said she was met by silence when she arrived. There wasn't even a god to greet her."

"That sounds like her – taking charge, ironic," said Hester.

"She said she didn't see a single soul in Heaven, just a lot of empty houses," Marty continued. "She thought souls would be wandering about like pigeons."

"Hah," said Bob.

"So, Heaven was out?" said Judy.

"Apparently."

"It was never possible to ignore her," said Debbie, another cousin. She sounded wistful. "Is that a good quality?"

"Probably not," said Maureen.

"She always felt that life was both surreal and real," said Hester. "And absurd."

"That's true."

"She was a great fan of clouds!" said Susan, Jean W.'s neighbour. "She said watching clouds gave her moments of serendipity she couldn't explain. She didn't know what those moments meant but she knew that they mattered."

"Put down clouds, Glen."

"Righty-o," said Glen, who was acting as secretary. Glen was Marty's friend.

"She was a big fan of rainwater, too, pools of it, splashing across the car windshield," said Margaret, Hester's wife.

"Rain, Glen."

"Got it."

"She could make you lose your mind laughing," said Karen, who was Jean W.'s friend from grade two. "One time. Oh, ha ha ha."

"This is like doing a post-mortem walkabout!" said Glen.

"Sometimes her path was marked with her most human tendencies," said Brenda, Jean W.'s spiritual guide. "For her children, especially, and for all animals."

"True again," said Marty. "She had a lot of startling moments in her life. It's shocking to realize how many."

"The world is so potent," said Brenda.

"So, we should focus on clouds?" said Glen.

"Clouds and rain and dogs and startling moments, I think," said Marty. "Anything else?"

"Mention her work," said Hester.

"And Marty and the kids and grandkids. And don't forget the rest of the family," said Debbie.

"Say she did what she could to change the atmosphere of people's days," said Hester.

"Love should be in there somewhere," said Karen.

"That's what I'm talking about," said Hester.

"Say she made a good pot roast," said Maureen.

"Say she died doing what she loved best, which is to say, living," said Bob.

"Good one," said Glen.

"Do you think she can hear us?" said Margaret. "I mean right now?"

"Of course she can hear us. I'm getting a very strong signal," said Brenda.

"You are? Boy, I'm kind of lit up by that!" said Glen.

"Jean W.! Knock three times on the wall if you can hear us," said Brenda.

"Oh for God's sake!" said Maureen.

"Shush!" said Glen. "Listen."

Mind

"Will you describe the great blank space in your mind?" the students asked their meditation teacher.

They'd been attending his sessions for several months and were sure he had important insights to offer.

The teacher said, "You want to know what my emptied mind looks like?"

"Yes," the students said, "we do."

The teacher, whose name was Stanley Precious, closed his eyes for several minutes. When he opened them he said, "All right. It's like the start of a jigsaw puzzle. The card table is empty save for the border of naked ladies with their breasts out."

Satisfyingly, the students gasped.

One Sausage's Quest to Discover
the Truth About His Existence

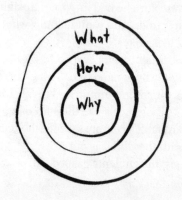

We turn up. We don't know
what the hell is going on.

1968

"Two images set side by side make a flash in the mind,"
said the English professor, "and this is what makes
poetry." He'd been talking about the twentieth century
Imagist poets.

"Such flashes," the professor said, "can produce
a dopamine rush. That's because we're encountering
something we haven't experienced before and, as a
result, we become highly delighted."

This is what happened to me that day in 1968, in
room 412, on the top floor of the Clearihue Building.
I got hit with the flash of understanding. There was a
sudden luminous cast to the air. It was magical. Looking
out the classroom window, I saw the far-off ocean, felt
a soft sea breeze. Then I noticed a couple on a balcony
across the way sharing a cigarette. This caused me
to think of exotic places – the South Pacific, North
Africa – and how one day I'd go to a place like that and
sit beneath a palm tree writing poems.

But others in the class said the flash was more like
being on a regular acid trip – swirling walls, impossible
colours, and all the rest.

Drizzle and Mist

An English pub.

A law firm.

A barbecue sauce.

A TV crime serial.

A pair of Yorkshire terriers.

A weather report.

A no-fun couple.

Your love affair.

The scene at home.

The name of a castle in a nineteenth-century novel.

A beer from Finland.

The name of the Little Prince's lost memoir.

The name of Sigmund Freud's lost theory.

The name of a painting bought at Sears in 1965.

Plastic Parts to Help with Life

We wanted to be in a happy place. So we bought a Lego
Farm set and moved in.

A Lego Farm is an environmentally friendly and
vegetarian farm where there are no slaughterhouses,
no feeding operations, no toxic lagoons, and no ill-paid
migrant workers. The sun is always shining and it's
always an optimistic day.

The set comes with a farmer, a young girl, a
farmhand, a yellow cat, a mouse, two brown-and-white
cows, five chickens, a Border collie, a riding mower, and
a tilting wagon.

In two hours we build the farmhouse. As long as
we're in this habitable zone, life is promising.

Before this, each of us was having upwards of
eighty bad moments a day. We called the ambulance a
lot and once Josh was airlifted to the hospital. When I
say bad moments I mean moments about seeing the
darkness, the sadness, and the bleakness of the world.
Moments on steroids, bigger and more dangerous than
regular moments, overtaking us like a drug.

Now we're feeding chickens and gathering pretend
eggs. Or wandering the farmyard, listening to the special
soundtrack that comes with the set. We put in the ear
buds and soon we're mooing along with the cows,
squawking with the chickens, and feeling pretty great –
privileged, on holiday, filled with fun.

Come evening we turn out the lights and everything
disappears – the night sky, our subterranean dread.
We're safe beneath a blanket of calm. We're not seeing
the billions of stars or thinking about their billions of
reasons. We're not losing our minds over the lunatic
moon. Because you know what happens if you fall in

love with moonlight, don't you? You end up living in cheap apartments forever.

Good thing we found this benevolent place.

And here comes the miniature farmer with good news, along with the miniature girl and the miniature aw-shucks farmhand, who once starred in *The Wizard of Oz*. We can build the mower! It's time to harvest the hay!

Finally, we're in a place that's just plain liveable. *Be happy for us, Marion, all right?*

The Lego instruction book guarantees that the farm figures will always be cute and silly enough to give us a thrill. That their plastic parts will remain durable. As long as we don't put the plastic parts in our mouths, we'll be safe. As long as we don't chew off the mouse's tail, all will be well.

Law of Supply and Demand

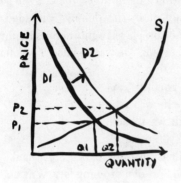

Some days, I'm like, can't we just have a regular conversation?

Protest

Bryce said to me during dinner, "You look like Jack Nicholson when you smile."

He was eating a hamburger; me, tomato soup.

"Jack Nicholson in *The Shining*," he added.

"Jack Nicholson played a murderous madman in that movie," I said. "He was so good it was hard to believe he was acting."

"He wasn't acting."

"Of course he was acting."

"That smile wasn't acting."

"What do you mean?"

"That smile is his trademark." Bryce said.

"It's awful. Sort of a drooling leer. Why do I look like him when I smile?"

"The smile's not that drooling."

"I get it. Saying I smile like Jack Nicholson is actually a pickup line. You want to pick me up. Now, while I'm eating tomato soup."

"It's an idea."

"You want to have one of those large moments where you lose yourself, where suddenly you don't know where you are?"

"I like those moments."

"And you think Jack Nicholson might be the key?"

"Possibly, yes."

Our conversation was interrupted by the protesters in the driveway. They're out there most nights. As usual they had their bullhorns and picket signs. They like to keep things current, so I wasn't surprised to see that tonight's protest was about Jack Nicholson's smile. "Down with drooling leers," they chanted. Rain flowed from the hoods and sleeves of their waterproof jackets.

"Oh you poor drenched things!" I cried, opening the door. "Come in, come in!"

I offered them tea and soup because the world had suddenly become a shaking monstrosity in need of care. But, no, the protesters said, they must press on. The night was long and there were many giants yet to slay.

Pressing Question

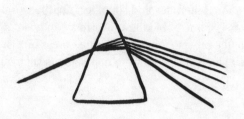

If we were to find life on another planet
and then die ourselves, would it be too
much to bear?

Lover of the Moon

I was having an early morning visit with my friend
Linda. We were sitting on her front steps sharing a
smoke. Darryl, her new "pet man," as she calls him,
joined us. Darryl, who is short and wide, was still in
his pyjamas.

"I'm a lover of the moon," he told me.

"Ah, yes, aren't we all?" I said, and looked at the sky.

"No really," said Darryl.

The moon was faintly visible at eight in the
morning, though it wasn't shining. "It looks like a
dull five-cent coin," I said. "You can see the outline of
a beaver."

"Oh no," said Darryl. "Just wait."

We watched the moon as strips of grey cloud drifted
across the sky. After a while the moon moved closer to us
and became a gigantic screen.

"Tell me the difference between the moon and a TV
set," Darryl said.

Linda said, "What did I tell you? He knows things."

I couldn't answer the question because I was
captivated. I watched the moon, as instructed, as if it
were a screen at an outdoor theatre.

Soon enough we could see advertising on the
moon's surface for a chain of hardware stores – a
salesman in a red shirt gesturing before a box of tools.
Then three young children eating cereal. After that the
cartoons began.

It was a muted moon. We couldn't hear a thing.

After Six Months

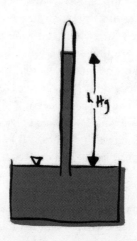

I got tossed into the deep end,
thanks to Howie.

Mud

I looked out our second-storey window and saw my grandfather trying to get in the basement door. What's he doing here? I wondered, and called my husband. "Eddy! Gramps is trying to get in the basement door!"

Eddy came running and had a look. "Well I'll be damned," he said.

We watched Gramps pull repeatedly on the door handle.

"He's supposed to be dead," said Eddy. "Do you think he got tired of it?"

"He did get bored easily," I said.

"What is it now? Fifteen years?"

"Seventeen. But he always was an active person. Remember the little bombs he'd make just for us?"

"He was cremated," said Eddy. "I can see him getting bored while underground, but cremated? I don't think boredom goes with that."

"There are some things we can't explain," I said. "I don't know what they are, but I know that they matter."

"I've heard that somewhere before."

By now Gramps was banging on the door with his fists. Then he slipped backwards into the mud that surrounds the basement step. He was wearing his beige windbreaker and blue plaid pants. They were smeared with mud.

We ran outside to see if he was dead again. He wasn't. He was mad.

"How many times have I told you to do something about that goddamned mud," he shouted.

The door he was trying to open belonged to the basement suite, the place he'd lived for seven years in the nineties. I had the awful feeling he wanted to move back in.

But the suite was rented now to a gentle recluse named Laura. Laura, of the permanently closed blinds and the stacks of newspapers and books forming delicate corridors through the rooms.

We left Gramps in the mud and went back inside. Still, I was worried. Once you are stuck in the mud, you are stuck in the mud, you know?

After lunch I looked out the window again. Gramps was still there so I opened the window and called out, trying for something that might catch him off guard.

"It's so great to see you," I said. "You look terrific! Congratulations on everything! We've always loved knowing you!"

This seemed to spook him. He vanished.

Transfer Problem

My neighbour, dead six weeks, visited me in the night
demanding money. He needed five thousand dollars, he
said, to keep the phantoms in Purgatory off his back. I've
always liked my neighbour – he once gave me three large
zucchinis from his garden – so I wanted to help.

The next morning I found a side street accounting
firm. My plan was to make a bank transfer. But it's
not as easy as you'd think. There are no banks in non-
existence, no procedures in place for transferring money
to a phantom.

The woman in the accounting office seemed
annoyed I'd even asked. She said, "I think your situation
will have a finale that you won't be pleased with."

Now I'm worried that my neighbour will visit again
and I'll have to admit defeat. He won't be happy. But
other than his chalk face staring at me and his bony
outstretched hand, what can he do?

"You think you've got problems?" I'll tell him.
"We're pretty sad up here about the gas bills we're
having to pay. We'd been running on vegetable oil for
years and then the rules got changed. And what about
Amy, who's no longer the beautiful peace rose she once
was? And the old dog and the cats with their vet bills?
And the burst water tank? God, don't you just hate how it
all goes on and on?"

Western Dreaming

In ten seconds the trouble was over, principally because there was no more trouble to make. At the big cave they tethered their horses. Then they got some boys to take their trunks over to the hotel.

Finally, they had the leisure to observe the effects that up to this moment they had avoided.

"I was behind that rock up there all the time," Lance said. "I had you covered."

"But Lance," Walleye asked, "what were them things falling out of the sky?"

"Comets," Lance said. "From another time."

Lance and Walleye started out the next day before the sun was hot. At the gulch they found Charlie Wilson lying on his face, shot through the back where they'd left him. For a moment this hit Walleye where he lived. Then a coyote barked sharply from a neighbouring hill and they moved on.

So the days passed wonderful.

As they rode, Lance would often remark to Walleye that, though he may not be successful in a star-forming region where our molecules are part of some final statement, he did know Paradise. It was the material right here. The sun mounting the sky each morning, the desert going silently through its changes.

Fallout from the Compassion Workshop

For several days after the workshop I began having other people's feelings.

My friend Chase's, a local filmmaker, for one. His feeling, now mine, was one of acute anxiety. He'd just completed his first feature-length documentary and was nervous about its reception. "Please like my film but I'm afraid you won't," his feeling said.

I couldn't eat for hours leading up to the screening in the basement of St. John's United Church. The film was about water. Still water, falling water, running water, grey-and-blue water, polluted water, rain water, water with white caps, water screaming from a tea kettle, toilet water when it's flushed. There was no music in the film, only the various sounds that water makes when it is moving and the long silences when it is not.

So I expected to feel Chase's happiness when the twenty or so people in the audience clapped after the film had ended, to feel his pleasure in their response.

But, instead, a different set of feelings intervened. It was Anne's irritability with John that overcame me. They'd been sitting in the row ahead of me for the viewing. She hated him. I felt sure of it.

The Notes Line Up

They sort of exist like pages in a book.
If you were to remove one of these pages,
the story would be lost. They are part
of the bigger picture and they all
have a reason.

An Octave Apart

He studied the progress of the uneventful
and was a celebrant of dead ends, loose
threads, black holes. She studied the
innumerable folds of her own childhood
but was often sick believing her life
had been uneventful. Frequently, he
gazed at her in perplexity. She avoided
his gaze, preferring to remain in a state
of stirring confusion. Somewhere in all this
the warming planet was noted, but
neither had the genius for a discussion
about that.

Many Happy Returns

At one o'clock in the morning the troubled neighbour boy phones to ask if he can sleep in our basement because his parents have kicked him out. We say yes.

The following morning the boy sets fire to the back lawn. It's summer, everything is dry, so it's easily burned.

We put out the fire. We want to help, so we let him stay for the day.

By late afternoon he's taken some drug that's transformed him into a seven-foot-tall man with tricks up his sleeve – the ability to create new dawns, for one. He does this by sliding a credit card into a cloud and shouting, "Ta-da!"

At that moment the day backs up and repeats itself, but this time it's a different version, lushly green where the original was burned and beige.

Soon young people dressed in swimsuits gather in our backyard for a summer barbecue. The tall man is flipping burgers. People are grooving on the dahlias, the rolling green lawn. There's birdsong and laughter.

No one is interested in the woman who yearns for better days. She's prostrate on the grass, arms around the tall man's leg, begging him for the use of his credit card.

It's Beginning to Promise a Happy Ending

He's wearing sunglasses, an army jacket, ripped jeans,
some high white boots. He's got that big hair. And we're
thinking, "This is great!"

So we have a party, wheel out a Welcome Home
cake. Just when we thought he'd become another
dope doing the *Titanic*, he's beginning to promise a
happy ending.

Now it's like everyone who's been placed in this
story is feeling better. Whereas before we didn't know
what the hell was going on.

So the official answer to your question is, yeah,
it looks like Dad is no longer a complete fucking
nightmare. Even though Mom is saying, "I'm going to
build my own Swiss Family Robinson tree fort and stay
there – I'm going to start building right now," the rest of
us are being charmed. Dad's hauled out his old guitar.
He's playing his favourite Dean Martin tune. *"When the
moon hits your eye like a big pizza pie,"* he's singing at us.
"When the stars make you drool ..."

"That's amore," we sing along, forgetting the
alcoholic waste of him.

Today's Mystery

Today you will watch a film showcasing people who are spokespersons for dirt.

The film is promoted as an "outside-the-box" film, suggesting that by watching it, viewers will embrace new ways of looking at its subject. Dirt will become meaningful in their lives, whereas now what are meaningful are pavement, roads, carpet, linoleum, and hardwood floors.

A white farmer from California will speak about sowing his soul each time he sows a seed. A woman from India will speak about dirt being the earth's skin.

A wine critic of Spanish descent will speak about tasting dirt from the region where the grapes are grown. He will demonstrate this by bending down beside a row of grapevines, taking up a handful of dirt, smelling it carefully, and then putting it in his mouth. After chewing thoughtfully for a few moments, and while still crouched with the sun dappling through the grape leaves, he will pronounce the dirt to be of excellent quality.

Watching, you will come to the realization that the film is like a dream in which the reason for the spokesperson's existence is unclear but nevertheless important.

Mystery Woman

In the parking lot there is wind and rain, but inside it is
better – polished floors and overhead lighting.

I am a mystery woman dressed in beige. I am
wearing a beige raincoat like a detective.

There aren't many shoppers in the mall on this
Tuesday morning. Clerks on their breaks gather at a
kiosk selling nail polish. To them I am not a mystery.
I am a beige woman of no interest.

I am of no interest to the clerks in Below the Belt,
either, who are standing catatonic beside tables of tank
tops, meditating, perhaps, on a different life.

In Payless ShoeSource I'm invisible. But listen
as a clerk cries false to her co-worker. "My life is not
supposed to be about wedge sandals and neon hair!"

In Virgin Plastics, science is on sale. The theory of
relativity is marked down eighty percent. The sale table's
a mess of broken *E*'s. But I'm bored with relativity, and
so is everyone else. The store's deserted. The clerk is
asleep behind the cash machine.

At eleven o'clock in the morning the Science
Guy makes a scheduled appearance at the Food Court.
There's a crowd of the very old to see him. Science Girls
radiating electric currents from their headbands hand
out information sheets about how a lightbulb works.

Who is dead here? I wonder. Who is alive? Am I
ghost shopping?

I move along.

The girl in Splash tells me a new swimsuit will
cause me to couple soon. I think about Randall at home
with his tin of tomato soup for lunch and his jigsaw
puzzle of Windsor Castle. I think, *probably not*.

Dot Block

Sometimes I feel I can't move beyond
my ladder of tones, says Big Dot.
    And then I remember the words
of Doris Lessing: "The conditions are
always difficult." And feel emboldened
and take heart and say to myself,
You've got to finish that Grand Partita!

She Didn't Like Boxes

The twentieth-century artist Georgia O'Keeffe said she
didn't like boxes. Didn't like it when men tried to put her in
a box. Didn't like it when women tried to put her in a box.

"When people see erotic symbols in my paintings,
they're really talking about their own affairs," she said.

O'Keeffe's affairs were multiple and varied. They
included flowers, mountains, lakes, patios, trees, the
Brooklyn Bridge, jawbones, fungus, and her occasional
husband, Alfred Stieglitz.

About enjoyment, she said, "I wish people were all
trees. I think I could enjoy them then," adding, "Not one
of my nicest thoughts."

For much of her creative life, O'Keeffe lived in New
Mexico. When she was eighty-five, she hired a young
sculptor, Juan Hamilton, to be her companion and
caregiver. He was twenty-seven at the time and remained
with her until she died at ninety-six.

No boxes for them.

The Short Plant Prize

The celebrated Australian actress Judy Davis appeared
in my living room in the middle of the night to give me
a prize. It was for a book I had written seventeen years
ago. I've always admired Judy Davis.

"The prize is late," she said, "but oh well."

A kind of ceremony was held in a corner of the
room. Only she and I were present, the others in the
house being asleep. We stood facing one another.
The mood was sombre.

To receive the prize, I had to read aloud from my
nominated book, *Where Does Creamed Corn Figure into
the Workings of the Universe?* I was nervous and excited
and couldn't decide on a passage, flipping through the
pages so many times that the book turned into a ball of
black string.

The prize was a short plant. But because my
book was now a ball of string, Judy Davis said it was
disqualified. She said she was sorry but the prize would,
instead, go to the next person on the list, one Fred J. Fast,
who had written something lively about bats.

"I don't think any reasonable person could have
predicted this outcome," I said.

"It's pretty common," said Judy Davis. "Leaves you
feeling like the world has cast you off, doesn't it? Like
you've been left in this weird confessional bubble."

Little Dot

When I'm playing the cello I call
my little dot and tell him I won't
be accessible for a few hours.

The Many Marions

I found a twenty-dollar bill on my latest trip to the tank.
This made me happy. Twenty dollars would get me a
double float. The tank was sitting on Marion Williams's
back lawn. She lives down the road. It was her turn to
host the tank. Beside the tank she'd set up a table with
champagne glasses filled with tank water. This time the
colour of the water was emerald green. Seven Marions
were standing around in evening clothes sipping
and chatting and occasionally saying, "Ah, the gentle
madness begins ..."

Marion Carlos Marion from next door was there in
her black silk bathing suit. She was already in the tank.
"Good for my parts of anguish," she said.

Marion Coburn was there as well. As usual she
was more interested in complaining about Marion
Whitehouse than floating in the tank or drinking the
water. Her complaint this time was about Marion's dogs.

Marion Coburn whispered to Marion Mac, "Marion
Whitehouse could see I was having trouble with Tazzie
jumping on Chiquita, and yet she did nothing. I feel it's
up to the owner to control their dog, especially when
the other one is on a lead, like mine was. Excuse my
language, but Marion W. did fart all!"

Old Marion Dickinson turned to Marion Coburn
and said, "You sound like an opera singer. I find them
silly. Their behaviour is like clucking chickens. Could
you speak in a normal way, please?"

Marion Dickinson is something of our leader.
Her three-hundred-year-old house is held together by
carpet ants holding hands, she says. And she loves
the tank water. "It gives you an experience not unlike
Transcendental Meditation. Remember that?"

Understandably, people are nervous about there being so many Marions in the neighbourhood. Three of us are recent widows. "Partners of Marions just seem to drop dead," they've been saying. "It's a risk being connected to one."

I declined a glass of the tank water, preferring, instead, the double float. Like the other Marions, I would get my dopamine hit in an amusement park of my own creation.

Later at home I hung a chandelier from the kitchen ceiling, loving life's levity like everyone else. Laurie eyed it warily. I hadn't installed it very well.

By next morning, he had packed the van and was gone.

My mother, another Marion, Marion Gibson, found me sobbing on the back porch.

"It's because of the tank, isn't it?" she said. "Oh, I understand! I understand those tears!"

Fugato for Five Dots

"In the dark times, will there also be singing?" asked Bertolt Brecht in a poem. "Yes," he answered, "there will also be singing about the dark times."

Notes

The opening epigraph by James Tate is from the poem "You Think You Know a Woman," in *The Eternal Ones of the Dream: Selected Poems, 1990–2010* (New York: HarperCollins, 2012).

"Positive Impact" uses quotes from an online Associated Press article by Kathy Willens titled "Millennials, Hoping to Find Connection, Ban the Booze," *NBC News*, March 28, 2017, accessed December 2018, https://www.nbcnews.com/better/wellness/millennials-hoping-find-real-connections-ban-booze-n739636.

"Thirty-Two Years On" depicts open and closed strings as hypothesized in string theory.

"The Missing Beacon" references *The Story of Sidney* by Peter Grant (London, ON: Porthole Press, 1998).

The diagram in "Thirteen Years with Myrna" is a simplified model taken out of classical electromagnetic theory.

The Henry David Thoreau quote in "One Alone" is from *Walden* (1854). The Al Purdy quote is from the poem "Man Without a Country" in *Piling Blood* (Toronto: McClelland & Stewart, 1984).

The "Self-Portrait" diagram is adapted from an instrument conceived by James Prescott Joule and used in nineteenth-century thermodynamics for measuring the mechanical equivalent of heat.

The Oscar Wilde aphorism in "The Happiness Seminar" appears in his *Epigrams: Phrases and Philosophies for the Use of the Young*, first published in 1894 in the Oxford University journal *The Chameleon*.

"The Merry Cemetery" references an online article by Christine Popp, "One of a Kind: Transylvania; The Merry Cemetery," *New York Times*, September 29, 2002, accessed December 2018, https://nyti.ms/2DFsieP.

The "Study of Contrasts" diagram is adapted from a visual comparison of "barrel"- and "pincushion"-type distortions in photographic lens (David Nichols, "Correcting Lens and Perspective Distortions," DMXzone, accessed December 2018, https://www.dmxzone.com/go/11397/correcting-lens-and-perspective-distortion/).

The opening sentences of "Her Cake" reference a Postmedia Network clip about aging.

"Happy New Year" originally appeared in *The Fiddlehead* 224 (Summer 2005), under the title "Now Is the Time," edited by Mark Jarman.

The poem "Mob of Good Old Boys" by James Tate, quoted in "Aria," is once again from *The Eternal Ones of the Dream: Selected Poems, 1990–2010*.

The "Law of Roundness" diagram is adapted from a two-dimensional representation of a Clebsch diagonal cubic surface, also called a Klein's icosahedral cubic surface, respectively named after German mathematicians Alfred Clebsch (1833–1872) and Felix Klein (1849–1925).

The "Law of Now" illustration is adapted from a comparison of two types of interactions as defined in quantum physics: a "worldline" (left), denoting a path, and a "worldsheet" (right), denoting a manifold.

"Seasonal Wonderment" references an online article by Danielle Gusmaroli, "Not swat she needed! Actress Nicole Kidman swallowed fly filming *Strangerland* in the parched Aussie Outback, director Kim Farrant reveals," *Daily Mail*, June 6, 2015, accessed December 2018, https://www.dailymail.co.uk/tvshowbiz/article-3113134/Nicole-Kidman-swallowed-fly-filming-Strangerland-parched-Aussie-Outback-director-Kim-Farrant-reveals.html.

The concentric circles in "One Sausage's Quest to Discover the Truth about His Existence" are inspired by Simon Sinek's "Golden Circle" model (startwithwhy.com).

"Plastic Parts to Help with Life" references, in the second paragraph only, *LEGO and Philosophy: Constructing Reality Brick by Brick*, edited by Roy T. Cook and Sondra Bacharach, Blackwell Philosophy and Pop Culture Series (Hoboken, NJ: John Wiley & Sons, 2017).

"Law of Supply and Demand" reproduces a classic supply-and-demand graph, where P = price, Q = quantity of goods, S = supply, and D = demand.

The "After Six Months" diagram is adapted from an illustrated explanation of a mercury barometer's operation.

"Western Dreaming" was inspired by the western novel *Arizona Nights* by Stewart Edward White (New York: Grosset & Dunlap, 1907).

"The Notes Line Up" and "Fugato for Five Dots" show a series of quarter notes with the following accent marks: from left to right, a dot or *staccato* mark, a *staccatissimo* mark, a vertical wedge or *marcato* mark, a horizontal wedge or *sforzato* mark, and a *tenuto* mark. "Dot Block" and "Little Dot" also depict a dot or *staccato* mark.

The Dean Martin song "That's Amore" in "It's Beginning to Promise a Happy Ending" is from the 1953 album *Dean Martin Sings* (Capitol Records).

"Today's Mystery" references the 2009 documentary film *Dirt! The Movie*, directed by Gene Rosow and Bill Benenson.

"The Short Plant Prize" makes a reference to a line spoken by Margaret Lanterman, better known as the Log Lady, in episode 9, "Coma," of the 1990–1991 TV series *Twin Peaks*, created by Mark Frost and David Lynch. The character was played by Catherine E. Coulson.

The Bertolt Brecht line in "Fugato for Five Dots" is taken from the short poem "Motto" in *Svendborg Poems* (1939); see "Later Svendborg Poems and Satires, 1936–1938" in the collection *Poems, 1913–1956*, edited by John Willett and Ralph Manheim with Erich Fried, Theatre Arts Books series (Abington-on-Thames, U.K.: Taylor & Francis, 1987), 320.

Acknowledgments

"Positive Impact," "The Weather Channel," and "Waiting Room" first appeared in *Geist* 108, Spring 2018, as "Stories from a West Coast Town." Grateful thanks to publisher and editor-in-chief AnnMarie MacKinnon and editor Michael Kozlowski.

The Walrus published stories and comics from the book in their December 2018 issue under the title "Plastic Parts to Help with Life" as follows: stories "In the Privacy of Their Own Condo," "Protest," "Lover of the Moon," "Fallout from the Compassion Workshop," "Plastic Parts to Help with Life"; comics "One Sausage's Quest to Discover the Truth about His Existence," "Thirty-Two Years On," "Six Months Later," and "Theory of Now." Great thanks to Jessica Johnson, executive editor and creative director, and to the *Walrus* team.

I am indebted to Kevin Williams, publisher of Talonbooks, for his continued support of my writing (*The Great Happiness* is my seventh book with Talon), to andrea bennett for her invaluable editorial advice and help with the graphics, and to Charles Simard for his sharp and engaging copy-editing. Talonbooks serves its authors exceptionally well and I am honoured to have my work published by them.

M.A.C. Farrant is the award-winning author of fifteen
works of fiction and non-fiction, a memoir, and two plays.

The Great Happiness: Stories and Comics is the third
part in her trilogy of miniature fiction. The first, *The
World Afloat: Miniatures* (Talonbooks, 2014), won the City
of Victoria Butler Book Prize for that year; the second,
The Days: Forecasts, Warnings, Advice (Talonbooks, 2016),
was nominated for both the City of Victoria Butler Book
Prize and the ReLit Award.

Farrant lives in North Saanich, British Columbia.